# THE SMELL OF COFFEE

## A. M. BURK

Written and Designed by A. M. Burk.
Cover Illustrated by Piarul Islam Pias.
Interior Illustrations by CatMadePattern.
Edited by Tim McKay.
Published by A. M. Burk LLC.
Copyright © 2026 A. M. Burk LLC. All rights reserved.



ISBN: 979-8-9910580-6-3
Library of Congress Control Number: 2026903030



First edition 2026

# 1. The Land of Memory

Christmas.

For most people, that single word brings to mind brightly colored lights, meticulously wrapped presents, peaceful Nativity scenes, and the love of family and friends.

Not for me.

For years, the very mention of the Christmas season would bring both a rush of excited chatter and a chorus of groans from me and my fellow classmates. For us, the Christmas season meant endless hours of grueling practice, high stress levels, friendly (and sometimes, not-so-friendly) competition, and the loss of any personal life until roughly mid-December... all in the hopes of bestowing a few magical nights upon others.

I am not a good writer. My older sister Marie always tells me that the written word is an art—a skill bestowed upon few in order to grace the world with their beautiful talent. She would often try to get me to join her in the literary world, but I would merely laugh. Although I would be the first to admit that her poetry is truly a work of art, I typically prefer to express my thoughts and emotions in a very different way—through ballet.

So, at this point, you probably have a lot of questions... Like why a twenty-year-old guy does ballet. Or why I am writing this when I've already established that I tend to shy away from the literary arts.

Why do I dance? I think that's actually one of the hardest questions anybody has ever asked me. Over the years, I have given many different answers to family, friends, guidance counselors, dance instructors, college admission counselors, and even to myself. However, I think the best possible answer is that I simply need to dance.

Dancing, to me, feels as natural as breathing... except it takes a lot more work. I started in ballet when Marie started, roughly fourteen years ago. My parents just didn't have the heart to tell their six-year-old son he couldn't start dance class with his big sister. They didn't realize how much that simple decision would change my life.

When you're a girl, everybody thinks it's cute to be involved in dance. However, the minute that a guy says he likes to dance, the tables turn. It's hard to describe what it's like to be a guy in ballet. Usually, people within the dance troupe are decently supportive. Sure, there's always a couple jerks who will make the assumption that I must be gay because I like ballet, but typically the other dancers are just happy to have a guy around for the lifts and duets.

It's really the people outside of the dance sphere that I have to be careful of. I won't repeat all the things that I have been called over the years, but the typical sentiment is the same: since I like to dance, I must be gay, rich, and a sissy who's never had to work for anything in his life. Just typing it, I feel the urge to laugh. People who think this clearly have never tried the extensive barre warm-ups my instructors tortured me with ever since I started. They will never know how grueling a day of practice can be, especially if the day involves a lot of lifts. They will never realize how it feels to have blood blisters on your feet from doing a move wrong or how it feels to wake up in a cold sweat after dreaming that your hands slipped and you dropped your duet partner.

But even if the stigma is wrong, it doesn't mean that it's not still there.

Marie dropped out eventually to pursue cheerleading, but I remained enamored with dance, particularly ballet.

Since male dancers are hard to come by, my instructors were more than pleased to encourage my passion and train me to the best of their abilities. And so, I flourished. The combination of sincere passion and intense methodical training showcased my natural talent, providing me with opportunities to study under some of the greatest minds in dance.

I danced whenever and wherever I could. Camps, exhibitions, master classes—you name it, I was there. While Marie was off studying English at Yale and my younger sister, Clara, was busy learning karate, I was poring over options that would allow me to continue dancing professionally. I knew my parents were concerned that their only son was throwing his life away on a whim, but I couldn't help it. To me, ballet was something beautiful and exotic that only seemed to show her face through sacrifices of sweat and pain. Dance entranced me, filling my dreams with hopes of professional solos and choreographing for the world's next generation of dancers.

My parents said they would always support me, but it wasn't until I was offered a rather large scholarship to study the performing arts at a prestigious university that they realized what I already knew: that dance was my life.

As far as why I am writing this... I am writing to remember. Someday, when my limbs can no longer carry me through the movements and rhythms of dance, I want to remember the lights, the sounds, the emotions. I want to remember the feeling of flying, of passion, of intensity.

I want to remember her.


What do you think of when you think of Christmas?

I think of an early December night.

I think of the smell of coffee.

# 2. The Audition

To anyone who has ever worked with an American ballet troupe, the mere whisper of the holiday season brings a single thought to mind: *"The Nutcracker."* By August or September, it always feels as though every ballet school has become consumed by the much-beloved Russian ballet. For some reason, the tale of the sweet, innocent Clara saving her beloved toy, only to have her nutcracker turn into a prince and, in turn, save her, has entranced generations around Christmas time. For me, the story always reminded me of new beginnings and that people are never quite what they initially seem.

Little did I realize how accurate that statement was.

This story begins in August of 2015—the start of my sophomore year of college. Like quite a few other schools, my university's major production of the fall semester was none other than Tchaikovsky's famed ballet. Auditions were held the first Saturday of the semester. I still remember standing in the bare hallway waiting for my name to be called. It was chilly that early morning, despite the crowd of people milling around. I could feel myself shivering and cursed thin ballet tights for not the first time in my life. I kept telling myself not to be nervous. I could count maybe three or four other guys in the crowded waiting area. Surely, I would be a shoo-in for a role... at least, that's what my parents kept assuring me.

"Ben Riolo."

Taking a deep breath, I pushed through the throng and found myself in the large audition hall. Strangely enough, the actual audition wasn't the most stressful part of the audition process. Don't get me wrong—I was so nervous I almost fumbled through the brisé that is usually my show-stopper. But hands down, the worst part of the whole thing was the waiting. Seriously, I feel like sometimes the casting directors just like to torture people.

Two weeks later, I heard a rumor while in my Intro to Choreography class. I could hardly focus for the remaining half hour of class. As soon as the professor shut down her computer, I was out of the room, trying in vain to control my fear and excitement. Sure enough, the whispers were true: the cast list for *The Nutcracker* was out. Holding my breath, I ran my finger down the long list of names. I knew I would never be cast for the role of the Cavalier, escort of the Sugar Plum Fairy; that was a role I knew the university reserved for the upperclassmen or special guest performers. Although I knew it was a long shot, I couldn't help but hope for the titular role. My heart beat faster as I briefly imagined myself calling my parents to tell them I had been cast as the Nutcracker. I could almost hear their proud voices congratulating me on my role.

Turning back to the cast list, I searched for my name with renewed vigor. Finally, I found it: *"Arabian Sultan/The Nutcracker Understudy: Ben Riolo."* My heart sank. I knew I should be happy about any role I received, but I couldn't help it. It's not that the "Arabian Sultan" wasn't a challenging role. It just wasn't... well-known.

I could hear the feigned enthusiasm in my parents' voices when I told them the role I was selected for. My poor mom, always trying to help, encouragingly told me, "Well, we can always hope that the boy playing the Nutcracker will get sick the night of the performance!"

Yeah... thanks, Mom.

Over the next several weeks, I devoted even more time than usual to my practicing. If I was to be the "Arabian Sultan," I was going to make sure I was the best

Arabian Sultan I could be. One night, I was practicing later than usual. I had just flunked a math test (curse you, College Algebra!) and I needed to blow off some steam before returning to my dorm room.

I was finishing my usual barre routine when I realized I wasn't alone. Turning around quickly, I saw an older woman standing in the doorway to the practice room. She was dressed simply in black with a thick, dark brown bun of hair perched precariously atop her head. Her face was lined and sharp, but her dark blue eyes held a bit of a sparkle as she watched my embarrassment when I realized that she had been watching me.

"Professor Zeigler," I said respectfully, giving her a little bow. This woman was the stuff of legend, in my mind at least. She had danced with the New York City Ballet for eight seasons and had been their prima donna for three seasons. She was well-known throughout the dancing community and the world for her meticulous pointe work and her methodical choreography. When I was in high school, I met her once at a summer camp where she provided the choreography for the summer ballet performance. Since then, I had been awe-struck.

Arianne Zeigler's work was, in all honesty, the reason I continued to study dance at the university level. Although I knew I would have still found a way to continue dancing, I also knew that money was sort of important if I wanted to be able to eat. I had been on the verge of seriously contemplating my parents' urgings to study business or something practical like that when I got to observe Ms. Zeigler choreograph. How she tackled each move and routine reminded me of a scientist; in her mind, each move needed to be exact, timed perfectly, and masterful. That was when I realized she had unknowingly provided me with the answer to my career dilemma.

After deciding to accept a large scholarship to the university, I was shocked and ecstatic to discover that Ms. Zeigler was one of the main ballet and choreography professors. A little later on, I was informed that, because of my desire to eventually form a career as a choreographer, Professor Zeigler would be my advisor.

To say I was excited would have been an understatement.

"I saw your audition."

I must have jumped because her mouth twitched as though trying to hide a smile.

"Why are you here?"

"I'm practicing, Professor."

Her mouth twitched again. "I can see that," she said wryly. There was a long pause. "Your audition was good."

I blinked, not sure if I heard her correctly.

This time she let out a barking laugh. "You look like a scared rabbit, Riolo. Relax!"

"S-sorry," I mumbled, feeling a flush come to my face.

"You wanted the Nutcracker role."

My flush deepened. "Yes, ma'am."

"You're a good dancer, Riolo," she continued, watching me carefully. "You have potential. I like your attitude at the barre."

I still couldn't believe my ears.

"They gave you the Sultan because you're still an underclassman. And you still need to work on your jumps," she added.

I could swear my ears were turning red.

"But, I still thought you could do it, which is why I made them pick you as the understudy. But," she held up a finger for emphasis, "it so happens that this is not the only *Nutcracker* performance I am choreographing."

"It's not?" My voice sounded squeaky in my ears.

"Nope," she said, popping the "p" for emphasis. "And I have an opening."

I froze, feeling my heart pounding in my chest.

"I need a Nutcracker."

I opened my mouth but nothing came out.

Her mouth twitched again. "So, what do you say, Riolo? You still want to play the Nutcracker?"

I could barely nod.

She gave me a genuine smile before returning to her usual business-like manner. "This Saturday at the Gaskell Dance Studio, nine a.m. sharp."

I swallowed. "Yes, ma'am." I hesitated. "A-and thank you."

She smiled again. "Just don't disappoint me. Now, get back to practicing. Your leaps will need to improve for your Nutcracker performance."

And that's how a twenty-year-old college sophomore was selected to play the Nutcracker in the community's Christmas ballet...

# 3. The Dancing Doll

"What am I doing here?" I muttered to myself, hoisting my dance bag a little higher onto my shoulder.

*"Dancing the role of the Nutcracker, making a good impression on Professor Zeigler, and adding to your skimpy resume,"* the oh-so-helpful voice in my head responded smugly.

"It's not skimpy," I growled to myself as I approached the large brick building in front of me. "It's just..." I struggled to find a better word, "...unfinished."

"Riolo!"

My head shot up to see Professor Zeigler standing outside by the entrance to the Gaskell Dance Studio.

"Glad to see that you could make it," she said tersely, shooting a glance at her wristwatch. "At least somebody's on time..."

Before I could ask anything more, she hurried me inside.

"Follow me," she said curtly, beckoning me to follow her into a spacious lobby and down a brightly lit hallway.

"So, is this a high school production?" I asked slowly as we passed several teenaged girls who giggled as they saw me.

"No," Professor Zeigler said brusquely. "My sister has a soft spot for anybody with a passion for dance, so she teaches anybody who wants to learn from the age of four up through high school."

"Wait," I said slowly. "This is your sister's school? I didn't even know you had a sister!"

The corner of Professor Zeigler's mouth twitched.

At that moment, a woman's voice rang through the corridor. "Arriane! In here!"

"This way." Professor Zeigler led me through the crowded hallway and into a large practice room where a tall woman with short light brown hair and bright blue eyes stood waiting.

"You must be Ben Riolo," the woman said, reaching out to shake my hand. "I'm Ms. Gaskell. Welcome to my school!"

"Thank you for having me," I responded politely, shifting my bag on my shoulder.

"My older sister has told me that you've got some remarkable talent!" Ms. Gaskell exclaimed.

"Please," scoffed Professor Zeigler, not looking at me. "Don't inflate his head."

Ms. Gaskell shot me a wink.

Within a few minutes, the room had gone from nearly empty to moderately full. Roughly fifty students of all ages had filed into the large practice room, some still yawning and blinking sleep back from their eyes.

"Alright, everybody! Listen up!"

Instantly, the room went silent. Every eye was fixed upon Ms. Gaskell as she welcomed them to the first official day of practice for *The Nutcracker*. I had been trying to stand off in a corner where nobody would notice me. That worked for about a whole five minutes while Ms. Gaskell went over her goals for the day and for the obligatory thanks to all the parents who allowed their children to participate.

"Now, I know you are all wondering who we have selected to play the Nutcracker," Ms. Gaskell continued. "As most of you are aware, we had not yet announced the dancer playing the lead role, because we were having trouble finding a student with the right... caliber for the practice schedule." It seemed to me as if this statement was pointed towards some guys in the back of the room who had been on their cellphones this entire time. "However, however," she continued, having to raise her voice slightly over the sudden outburst of whispering and quiet chatter at this announcement, "I am happy to announce that we have cast our Nutcracker."

My blood ran cold as Professor Zeigler motioned for me to join them at the front of the room. Although I liked dancing, being the center of attention when not on a stage was another matter entirely. I could feel my palms sweating and itching as I made my way to the front of the room. As if through a heavy fog, I distantly heard Professor Zeigler introducing me and I awkwardly waved at the group of students before me. Some of the younger ones waved back, putting me a little more at ease. I took a deep breath and relaxed.

After a few more minutes of going over the plan for the day, Ms. Gaskell dismissed the students to their various groups.

After a few awkward moments of pondering my current situation, I approached Ms. Gaskell. "Um, where should I go?"

The instructor smiled at me in her friendly, kind manner. "I think, this morning, I will just show you around the place and then let you help out with our 'mouse dancers.' That's our four to six-year-old group, and I could always use an extra hand." She sighed.

"Sure, I can help," I said, hoping I sounded confident.

"Then, in the afternoon, after most of the little ones have gone home, I'll see how much of my sister's choreography for the Nutcracker you already know."

"Ms. Gaskell?" A little girl about six years old ran over and gently tugged on her hand. "Ms. Lindsey's not here."

Ms. Gaskell frowned. "That's Lindsey Von Ballen—our girl who'll be playing the role of Clara," she explained to me. "What do you mean she's not here, Nessa?"

As if right on cue, the girl in question walked into the practice room, talking loudly on her phone as she did so. "Look, Monica, I'll have to call you back after practice," she said quickly, noticing Professor Zeigler's and Ms. Gaskell's irritated expressions. Hastily shoving her phone into her purse, she quickly took a seat. "I'm so sorry, Ms. Gaskell! I thought this thing started at 9:15!" she exclaimed in a tone of mock worry that set my teeth on edge.

"Of course you did," Ms. Gaskell sighed as though this was a recurring experience. "And you know that it's currently 9:30, right?"

My parents had always been really good about insisting that my sisters and I give almost everybody a chance. If I had even a penny for every time my mom started to say, "Now, you can't judge a book by its cover," I probably wouldn't have needed a scholarship to study dance. I tended to think I was pretty good at giving everybody the benefit of the doubt; after all, I, as a male dancer, had experienced the consequences of negative stereotypes firsthand.

That being said, it didn't take me long to come to the conclusion that I didn't like this Lindsey Von Ballen, the star of the show, or as I referred to her in my head, the "Barbie girl." At first, I really wasn't trying to be mean. Not in the least. But honestly, she looked like a real-life Barbie. She was probably around fourteen or fifteen and had long, very straight platinum blonde hair that she kept up in a tall ponytail. It appeared that everything she owned was in the same matching pastel purple color, whether that was her cell phone case, her gym bag, or even her dance leotard.

After we were introduced, Ms. Gaskell asked if Lindsey would like to show me around the studio, seeing as the pair of us would "be spending a lot of time together over the next few months." Lindsey readily agreed, her ponytail bobbing as she nodded and giggled in excitement. I shot a glance at Professor Zeigler, silently begging her to rescue me. To my dismay, Professor Zeigler merely gave me a stern look as if to say, "This is what you signed up for."

Inwardly bemoaning my situation, I reluctantly followed the girl out of the main dance room and down a corridor. For twenty minutes, I followed Lindsey as she showed me the various dance studio rooms. I had to admit: I was impressed. The studio was a lot larger than I was originally anticipating. I was just about to ask "Clara" how many students the school had enrolled when she cut me off.

"So, are you single?"

I stopped in my tracks, not quite believing what I heard. "Excuse me?"

Lindsey turned around, her blonde hair swishing around her face. She pursed her lips and batted her eyelashes in a way I assumed was supposed to be attractive. "Are. You. Single?" She repeated, enunciating each word with annoying clarity.

As it so happened, I was single. Extremely single. Like the kind of single guy all the girls would gang up on but not actually want to date. Like the kind of single guy who was teased incessantly about it by the few non-dance friends he had. But there was no way in heck I was going to let the walking, talking Barbie know that.

"I'm a college student!" I exclaimed incredulously. "You're what? Fourteen?"

She rolled her eyes. "Sixteen. Do keep up. Now, please answer the question."

"None. Of. Your. Business."

She smirked at me in that annoyingly plastic fashion that I was starting to associate with her. "I was just being friendly! After all, I am the prima donna, and you are the prince."

I could feel my blood begin to boil. I looked up to see Professor Zeigler watching us from down the hallway. I took a deep breath and smiled back at the blonde in front of me. "I'm sorry. I could have sworn that the Sugar Plum Fairy was the prima donna role in this performance," I flashed her a fake smile. "I have to run. Nice meeting you!" I called over my shoulder to the fuming girl as I made my way towards Professor Zeigler.

"Making some new friends?" Professor Zeigler asked dryly, watching me closely.

"Something like that," I admitted, not quite meeting her eye.

"Hmm."

Man, I had forgotten how annoying high school had been...

# 4. The Girl in the Spare Practice Room

The next few months were busy to say the least. By mid-October, I was starting to regret agreeing to dance in two separate productions. What little time I usually had after classes was now divided between homework and the practice rooms. Eventually, I started to fall into a routine. After classes, I would work on homework for a couple of hours before heading to the practice rooms at my university to work on the Arabian dances with my partner Jill, a Junior exchange student from Brazil. In the early evening, I would head home and have a hurried meal with my parents before heading back out to Ms. Gaskell's studio. Typically, I would stay there late into the night, practicing my solos as the Nutcracker and attempting to perfect my leaps.

My weekends were nonexistent as I vainly tried to make all the practices for both performances. Quickly, my somewhat healthy lifestyle evolved into a daily nightmare of hours of intense practice, very few hours of sleep, meals consisting entirely of cold sandwiches and energy drinks, and a general spiral into insanity. Eventually, Professor Zeigler had to take me aside and give me a lecture over how idiotic I was for "working myself to oblivion." As much as I wish I had handled that comment with poise and grace, I think my response was more along the lines of "Well, isn't that what you had to do to get where you wanted to be?" ... except a little less polite and quite a bit more sassy. My face burns just to think of it, but at that point, exhaustion and caffeine were controlling what little rationality I had left.

When Professor Zeigler merely smiled at me and her eyes ceased their cheery twinkling, I realized that I had gone too far. The next two hours were spent performing drill after drill after drill until my legs were shaking from the exertion and my head was spinning from exhaustion. Finally, she allowed me to sit. Gratefully, I slumped against the wall, my muscles still trembling.

"Riolo."

Slowly, I looked up and met her eyes, dreading what she was about to say.

She looked down at me, a strange expression in her eyes. I will never forget what she said next.

"You can't dance if you are dead," she said simply. Without another word, she turned and left me alone with her words.

Ever since that night, my practice routine changed drastically. Don't get me wrong, my practice schedule was still more chaotic and ridiculous than it really should have been. But at least now, I was usually getting at least five hours of sleep and I was forcing myself to take more than five or six minutes for meal breaks.

Most nights, I would still remain at Ms. Gaskell's studio long after dark, hoping that, when those fateful December nights came, I would be ready. One night, in particular, I had been practicing hard and felt that I had finally gotten my brisés into a form that even Professor Zeigler would be proud of. Looking up at the clock, I realized it was still early in the night and decided to do something crazy, something rash, something completely out of the ordinary for "high-achiever, honor student, Ben Riolo."

I decided I would call it an early night.

As I walked down the hallway towards the studio's exit, I saw something out of the corner of my eye and I froze. Silently, I retraced my steps, stopping finally outside of an empty practice room. Or at least, I initially thought it was empty...

As I surreptitiously peered into the small room, I heard gentle music begin to play. It only took a moment for me to recognize it: "The Waltz of the Snowflakes". Suddenly, a small figure gracefully leapt into the air. I felt my breath catch as I watched silently, privy to a truly magical sight. As the music swayed gently, I saw a single dancer practicing, her head bowed in concentration as she counted quietly aloud to herself.

She was tall for a ballerina, I realized as I watched her. However, her body was lithe and lean, toned from clearly many years of intense training. She was by no means a newcomer to ballet, I realized, as she seamlessly moved into a tricky pointe routine. She moved with a grace and poise of which I found myself envious. As she danced, she made it seem maddeningly easy while still somehow breathtakingly stunning. Although I knew she was merely practicing one role in a piece that typically utilized twelve or so performers, she seemed to dance as though preparing for a solo.

I'm not sure how long I watched. As she seamlessly moved through her transitions, I realized that I had quickly become entranced. This strange girl was a drug—no matter what I did, I couldn't tear my eyes away from the beautiful auburn-haired ballerina. I wondered what her name was, for I knew I had never met this girl before. I considered walking in and introducing myself, but at the mere thought of interrupting the ballerina, my mouth went suddenly very dry and my knees felt strangely weak.

As a final triumphant fanfare blared from the stereo in the corner, the ballerina gracefully slid from a final en pointe position into a beautiful curtsy. It seemed as though that moment was frozen in time. All that mattered was the breathtaking girl who remained as still as a statue. And then in an instant, the moment was gone.

As the girl got to her feet, a sudden panic overwhelmed me. Without even truly thinking it through, I bolted. I didn't stop running until I found myself in the parking lot of the dance school. I leaned up against the outside wall, feeling the chilly evening breeze blow against my flustered face. My heart was still pounding, even as I attempted to nonchalantly walk across the parking lot to my little, run-down car.

I must have still appeared flustered when I arrived back home, because my mother noticed that my cheeks were red and was convinced I must be ill. I tried to reassure her that I was perfectly healthy and that she needn't worry... which was probably the worst thing I could have done, because it seemed to make her worry all the more. To soothe her fears, I promised her that I would go to bed early and try to take it easy over the next few days.

However, as I lay in my bed that night, I realized that I may have accidentally made a promise to my mother I would be unable to keep. For every time I closed my eyes, all I could see was the slight figure of a ballerina with thick, auburn hair.

# 5. Of Pneumonia and of Propositions

Change.

It's a necessary part of life.

But it's never supposed to happen a week before a major production.

My university's production of *The Nutcracker* finished up after three performances during the Thanksgiving weekend so as to provide all of the exhausted ballet students a chance to study before the onslaught of finals. While I, like my fellow colleagues, was quite content with this arrangement, I was happy for a completely different reason. With the university performance out of the way, I could focus solely on Ms. Gaskell's performance.

Don't get me wrong—I enjoyed dancing as the Arabian Sultan. For those of you who may not be familiar with this role, the Arabian Sultan is one of two dancers who represent the coffee of Arabia. After the Nutcracker saves Clara from the Mouse King and transforms into a prince, he takes her to his home: the Land of Sweets. To honor the bravery and resilience of Clara, the ruler of the Land of Sweets, the beautiful Sugar Plum Fairy, brings out a number of performers to dance for Clara, each representing some delectable sweet from various parts of the world. These sets of dances are usually technically challenging and somewhat flashy, as they are meant to impress the young Clara. The Arabian dance is no exception.

The dance partners representing the Arabian coffee typically only dance a few times in the background aside from the Arabian Pas de Deux (a type of intricate duet that is well known for showcasing the talent and passion of its participants). In *The Nutcracker*, the Arabian Pas de Deux is well-respected among ballet dancers for being technically challenging, usually ranking just behind the Grand Pas de Deuxs of Clara and the Nutcracker and of the Sugar Plum Fairy and her Cavalier in terms of difficulty. In stark contrast to the cheery and playful dances of the Spanish chocolates and the Chinese tea, the Arabian Pas de Deux is an intense, sensual performance, usually relying on the extreme flexibility, agility, and passion of the performers.

Or it would if the performers had passion.

My experience dancing as the Arabian Sultan for my university was definitely a challenge, but it was likewise a bit of a disappointment. I mean, my partner Jill and I danced well—our techniques were excellent, our timing perfect, our lifts flawless. Yet, somehow, our performance suffered. It felt mechanical dancing with Jill and, although I truly tried my best, I know it showed. The passion, the sensual desire, the elegance were all nonexistent.

With that performance now out of the way, I was eager to devote the majority of my attention to the role of the Nutcracker. I told myself that my sudden desire to be impeccable in my dancing techniques as the Nutcracker was because of the rumor buzzing through Ms. Gaskell's school that some professional talent scouts would be in attendance for the performance. However, I knew I was kidding myself if I thought that was the real reason I wanted to blow everyone out of the water that December weekend.

The real reason had to do with a mysterious copper-haired ballerina.

Despite all of my not-so-sneaky attempts to catch a glimpse of her again, our paths never seemed to cross. I didn't even know her name. The only thing I knew was that she was a member of the Snow Corps since I had seen her practicing "The Waltz of the Snowflakes." Although I tried discreetly to figure out the names of everyone in the Snow Corps, I quickly discovered that some of the younger ballerinas found my curiosity a bit... unnerving.

In the long run, though, I realized it wouldn't matter terribly. I would see her again at least for the dress rehearsal and the performance. In the meantime, I would simply practice as much as possible so that I could hopefully impress and intrigue her when our paths next crossed.

Eight days before the opening night of Ms. Gaskell's performance, I was summoned to Ms. Gaskell's studio for an "urgent meeting." Assuming it was something along the lines of "I need some extra help teaching the five-year-olds their routines," I naturally obliged. When I approached her little office in the corner of her studio and heard raised voices, I began to wonder what I had gotten myself into...

The voices suddenly stopped as I knocked on the door. A moment later, a very frazzled looking Ms. Gaskell appeared in the doorway.

"Ben! Please, do come in!" she said with a sigh of relief, ushering me into her small office.

"Benny, say you won't do it!"

I didn't even have to look to know who had just thrown her arms around me.

"Seriously, I don't think I even have to hear what it is; I'll do it!" I muttered, disentangling the girl's arms from around my waist.

After our first... uncomfortable meeting, I had hoped that Lindsey Von Ballen would eventually shed the popular girl act and at least become tolerable to work with.

Boy, was I wrong.

Within a week, *someone* had started rumors that the two of us were dating. Within two weeks, she had started calling me "Benny," despite my insistence that my parents had actually given me the name "Ben," not "Benny." Before three weeks were up, I was actively trying to avoid her at all times other than our mandatory practices for the duet pieces.

"Riolo." I turned to see Professor Zeigler give me a curt nod from a corner of the office. I couldn't help but notice the bright pink flush in her cheeks and the cold glint in her eyes as she stared down Lindsey from across the room. Brushing a few stray hairs away from her face, the seasoned ballerina appeared strangely out of breath, leading me to wonder if she had been the one shouting.

"Benny—"

"It's Ben."

"—they want you to give up the Nutcracker role! They want to steal your spotlight away from you and your princess!" she whined, batting her annoying blue eyes up at me.

"Last I checked, I don't dance with a princess," I said coolly, crossing my arms and glaring at her. However, my blood ran cold at her words.

"Stop being so dramatic," Professor Zeigler snapped, tapping her foot dangerously.

Ms. Gaskell shot her sister a warning look. "Lindsey," she said gently, turning to the distraught girl, "if you had been listening, you would have realized that we were suggesting no such thing."

"No offense," I finally cut in, "but I'm pretty confused right now."

Ms. Gaskell let out a sigh and turned back to me with a small smile. "Unfortunately, Colin Feln, our Arabian Sultan, was just hospitalized for pneumonia."

"Oh." Somehow, that was the most articulate answer I could come up with.

"We want you to dance the Sultan, in addition to the Nutcracker," Professor Zeigler stated, taking a step forward. "I've watched you practicing for the Arabian Pas de Deux and you know the routine backwards and forwards. The choreography is identical to your last performance since I was in charge of both."

I swallowed hard, my mouth very dry. "But, Professor, how could I dance two roles at once?"

"We talked about that." Ms. Gaskell motioned for me to take a seat in the only unoccupied seat in the room. "The Nutcracker usually stands on stage with Clara during the presentation of the sweets before rejoining her for the Final Waltz. My sister and I agree—we could easily sneak you off stage before or during the entrance of the Spanish dancers. You would quickly change costumes, meet up with Mina, perform the Arabian Pas de Deux, change back to the Nutcracker costume, and be back on stage in time for the finale." I must have looked nervous because Ms. Gaskell quickly added, "But we aren't forcing you to do this, Ben. If you don't want to, we would understand."

"But we really don't have any other options," Professor Zeigler pointed out grimly. "As you may have figured out, Riolo, we don't exactly have a surplus of male dancers."

As I stifled a laugh, Lindsey jumped once more to her feet, her hands planted firmly on her waist. "Of course, he doesn't want to do it! He's already my partner! Why would he want to dance with someone else?"

"I'll do it." Everybody turned to look at me; Lindsey's jaw dropped. "You convinced me, Lindsey. Any opportunity to dance with someone else would be welcomed."

Professor Zeigler let out a loud, barking laugh as Lindsey turned very red and began yelling obscenities at me. Honestly, I wasn't even sure most of what she said until after she had spun on her heel and marched out of the room.

"That wasn't very tactful, Arianne," Ms. Gaskell said reproachfully, glaring at her sister.

Professor Zeigler scoffed. "She's just jealous, that's all. She can't stand the thought of Riolo dancing with Durand."

"Is Durand the name of the girl I'll be dancing with?" I asked curiously.

"Yes," Ms. Gaskell affirmed, rubbing her temples as if to ward off a headache. "Mina Durand is one of our star ballerinas. She's a high-school junior this year. I think she may have a shot at dancing professionally, if she ever wants to. She's actually starred as Clara in our last two performances. She declined to star again so as to give another ballerina a chance."

"You'll like her, Riolo. She works hard," Professor Zeigler stated in what I assumed was meant to be an encouraging tone.

"We'll have to get a lot of practicing in; the Arabian Pas de Deux is tricky," I muttered, cursing myself for agreeing to dance with yet another emotional high schooler. Although the look on Lindsey's face had been priceless, I realized that it may not have been smart to agree to dance two different roles in the same production only to infuriate her.

"Don't worry," Professor Zeigler said with a wry chuckle. "I think she'll surprise you."

"Well, come on then!" Ms. Gaskell beamed, taking me by the arm. "With only a week to go, we haven't much time to waste!"

What did I get myself into?

# 6. Through Deep Water

I was still regretting my rash decision as I followed Ms. Gaskell down the long corridor towards the main practice room. I had been so relieved to finish up one of the productions and here I was about to start practicing for another role in *The Nutcracker*. I silently vowed that this would be the last *Nutcracker* production I would ever allow myself to get roped into.

As we approached the practice room, I heard a beautiful lilting melody drifting from the open practice room. Although I recognized it as being from *The Nutcracker*, the name of the piece escaped my mind.

"As you may have noticed, we are a bit limited on talented performers here," Ms. Gaskell mentioned in an apologetic tone. "Mina is one of our best ballerinas, so she has graciously agreed to perform in the Arabian dance and as part of our Flower Corps and our Snow Corps."

If Ms. Gaskell continued to speak, I was unaware of it, for at that moment we entered the practice room and I suddenly found myself unable to move.

There, on the other side of the room, stood the girl who had entranced me a little more than a month before. She was dancing along to the music, seemingly oblivious to the fact that she was no longer alone. A small smile spread across her face as she moved with ease into a demi-pointe pirouette. I could have easily stood there and watched her graceful, intoxicating movements all day...

At that moment, the music suddenly stopped, shattering the dream I had been drinking in. The girl stopped partway through a series of entrechat quatres[1], looking up to see what had caused her music to cease. As she lifted her head, I realized I had never seen her eyes before. They were large and almond-shaped, framed by long, dark lashes. The color reminded me of freshly brewed coffee, dark and brown and rich. Her facial features were striking, with a very distinctly sculpted jaw and cheeks. She reminded me of royalty as she stood

---

1 A leap into the air from a position in which the legs are crossed, crossing and uncrossing the legs twice in midair, before finally landing with the legs crossed.

there surveying the room, a hint of confusion barely perceptible in her gorgeous face.

"Ms. Gaskell? Is something wrong?"

If it wasn't considered unmanly to swoon, I probably would have done so at this point. Her voice was... different. It was clear that she wasn't from this part of the world, but I was never very good at identifying accents. If push came to shove, I would probably guess perhaps British or German. Overall, the accent was faint, not enough to affect the clarity of her speech but only enough to add to her overall elegance.

"Sorry to interrupt you, Mina," Ms. Gaskell responded as she finished fiddling with the speaker to the far side of the room. "I mentioned earlier that we had a person who might be able to fill in for Colin? Meet Ben Riolo."

I awkwardly held out my hand. "Hello," I mumbled, my tongue feeling heavy.

Brushing her auburn hair out of her eyes, she gave me a truly breathtaking smile. "Hello, Mr. Riolo!" she said cheerfully, shaking my hand politely. "You're our guest performer, aren't you? You're Ms. Zeigler's pupil?"

"Yes, I mean, um. Yes," I finished lamely, cursing my brain for not wanting to work.

She giggled.

"Ben has already performed the role of the Arabian Sultan for another production earlier this year under my sister's guidance, and he is well-acquainted with the choreography you have been practicing," Ms. Gaskell remarked with a genuine smile.

"Really?" Mina's eyes lit up. "Oh, that's a relief! It would have been difficult for either one of us to learn a completely new routine in a week."

Still not trusting my body, I merely nodded and tried my best to give her a smile. I realized, despite all my daydreams of impressing this beautiful girl, now that she was standing before me, I probably looked more like a scared turtle than an impressive Nutcracker prince.

A clap behind me caused me to jump. Professor Zeigler stood in the doorway, surveying the scene with satisfaction. "Well, then, now that the pleasantries are out of the way, let's get working!"

The next several hours went by in a nerve-wracking blur. I quickly realized that Professor Zeigler and Ms. Gaskell were right: not only was Mina Durand an amazing performer, she also strove to be the very best that she could be. Whenever one of the sisters would stop the music to point out a misstep or a needed change in position, she would always listen intently before attempting her hardest to correct the mistake.

I wish I could say that I had as easy of a time correcting myself as Mina did. While we practiced, I felt as though I was moving through deep water. I sometimes found it hard to concentrate on Professor Zeigler's instructions and on Ms. Gaskell's pointers through the loud pounding of my heart in my ears. My hands were continually sweating, making the lifts even more nerve-wracking than usual. I was fidgety and jumped at any sudden movements.

Seriously, what had this girl done to me?

"Hey."

Ms. Gaskell had graciously given us a five minute break to get a drink when someone came up behind me. I jumped, almost spilling water all over me.

"Sorry," Mina said, pushing a loose strand of her copper hair behind her ear. "I didn't mean to startle you."

"Um—yeah—no! It's no big deal!" I blurted out, stumbling over my words and internally screaming at myself.

"Well, um, look, I just wanted to say that, you know, you can relax around me."

I blinked in confusion.

Mina let out an adorable laugh. "You don't talk much, do you, Ben?"

"Um—Well, I can," I managed to say slowly.

"Seriously, just relax! I promise I don't bite!" She smiled at me and I think my heart melted. She giggled again.

"What?" I asked curiously, feeling my ears turn red.

"It's just—everyone thinks that *I'm* the shy one. I can't believe I've found someone even quieter than I am!"

"Riolo! Durand!"

"Coming, Ms. Zeigler!" Mina called over her shoulder. "Just relax and do your best," she said encouragingly, giving me a pat on the arm. "You're a really good dancer!" she added as she walked back towards the barre.

I stood there frozen. I was sure that the blush from my ears was now spreading down my face.

"RIOLO!"

"Coming!"

# 7. All Dressed Up With Nowhere to Go

"This is ridiculous."

One of the seamstresses shushed me as she finished making the last adjustments to the Nutcracker's signature red jacket.

"How on earth am I supposed to see out of this thing, let alone dance?" I wondered, picking up the large, ornate Nutcracker head. I had seen performances of *The Nutcracker* before, obviously, but it never struck me that the dancers had to learn to dance while wearing the large costume heads.

"And that, Riolo, is why we are having a dress rehearsal," snapped Professor Zeigler as she entered the backstage costume area of the high school auditorium, her arms full of various papers and diagrams.

"Well, at least my relief at being transformed into the Prince will be genuine," I muttered under my breath, giving the Nutcracker head a stern glare.

"I heard that!" she barked back at me as she turned to leave the room.

It wasn't even nine in the morning, and I could tell that we were all off to a stellar day.

"Oooh, Benny!" came a squeal from behind me.

I closed my eyes. "It's too early for this, Lindsey. I can't handle you yet this morning."

She pretended not to notice me and instead was examining my Nutcracker costume. "You're going to look like such a handsome prince!" she giggled, twirling around with my boots.

"What are you? Twelve?" I snapped, snatching them back.

I could have sworn I heard a giggle from the seamstress as she finished up the adjustments. "There you go!" the woman said cheerfully, handing the jacket back to me.

The red and gold jacket was my favorite part of the ensemble, truth be told. The boots weren't half bad, but I had never been a fan of tights, especially the white ones that I had been assured were a "necessary part of the

46

Nutcracker ensemble." I also liked the sword I got to carry but it wasn't particularly flashy.

"Ten minutes!" Ms. Gaskell called out, sticking her head through the door to the costuming area. "Hurry up, everyone, please!"

With a grateful nod to all the seamstresses, I quickly got changed and ready. I had more time than most since I didn't officially come on stage until roughly a third of the way into the performance. However, my years of training had taught me that it was always good to observe the full dress rehearsal, if possible. It taught you a lot about what could possibly go wrong and where the stumbling points for the entire production were most likely going to be.

Twenty minutes into the dress rehearsal, it quickly became obvious what the production's biggest roadblock was going to be: Lindsey Von Barbie. Whether it was arguing with the poor boy who was playing Fritz or rudely pointing out where other people were failing, the prima donna made it clear that she believed she was running the show, much to the frustration of Ms. Gaskell, Professor Zeigler, and, well, everybody else. It finally took Professor Zeigler threatening to kick her out of the performance, prima donna or not, to get her to be quiet, although she continued to sulk throughout the rehearsal.

Surprisingly enough, our duets actually didn't go over quite as badly as I was expecting. Despite all of her unlikeable traits, Lindsey really wasn't a horrible dancer and, thankfully, she had been practicing. I was feeling pretty good with our performance until Ms. Gaskell suddenly stopped us partway through the Grand Pas De Deux at the start of Act 2.

"You two are dancing well, but you're both forgetting something, especially you, Ben."

"What?" I asked, confused. I knew this routine backwards and forwards. What was I doing wrong?

Ms. Gaskell sighed, pushing a pair of reading glasses up a little higher onto her face. "Clara was just saved by the Nutcracker and, in turn, saved the Nutcracker by throwing her shoe and killing the Mouse King. Now, he's taking her back to his kingdom to show her off to his people."

I frowned. "Ms. Gaskell, I don't think I understand what I'm forgetting. I know the story of *The Nutcracker.*"

"Well, by this point, the Nutcracker and Clara are definitely in love with, or at least, attracted to one another."

I nearly choked.

Lindsey gave me a coy smile.

I growled under my breath. "You little—"

"Manners, Benny," Lindsey whispered with a smirk, batting her eyelashes.

Ms. Gaskell made us do the whole scene over again. I forced myself to smile through the performance, although to me, our dancing seemed cold and harsh.

"Stop." Ms. Gaskell ran her fingers through her hair. "That was much better, Lindsey. Ben—" she hesitated. "At least this time you were smiling," she finished finally. "Just keep trying."

I gave her a curt nod and started counting down minutes until I could leave the stage (and Lindsey's presence) to change for the Arabian dance.

Finally, at about an hour into the run-through, it was time for me to slip away from the stage under the cover of the entrance of the Spanish dancers. Thankfully for me, the Arabian costume was much simpler than that of the Nutcracker. In an effort to make changing costumes easier, the Arabian costume was merely a pair of loose red pants with gold embroidery and a pair of golden upper arm bands. Peering at myself in the mirror, I quickly attempted to get my light brown hair to lie flat. Although I was somewhat self-conscious about dancing bare-chested, I quickly reasoned with myself that anything had to be better than dancing in the Nutcracker head.

Hurrying back to the wings off-stage, I tried to get myself mentally ready for the Arabian performance. I was determined that this performance, I would do it—I would master the sultry, captivating role of the Arabian Sultan. I had actually convinced myself I could pull it off... until I caught sight of Mina.

This time I know my face must have turned beet red.

Her costume was designed to match mine. She was also wearing red, loose pants that came down to just above her pointe shoes. She had a golden sash tied around her waist that seemed to float whenever she moved. Her midriff was bare below a red and gold sequined top that sparkled in the lights backstage. Her auburn hair was twisted into an elegant bun beneath a simple golden tiara.

Turning, she saw me gaping at her. "Well, how do I look?" she asked nervously.

"You—" I paused, thinking. She looked breathtaking, stunning, gorgeous. But none of those words seemed to fully convey what I wanted to say.

"You—" I tried again, taking a deep breath. I suddenly frowned and took a sniff. "You—You smell like coffee."

She let out a loud laugh and quickly attempted to stifle it before Professor Zeigler could call us out. Choking back her laughter, she finally managed to say, "I'm afraid that wasn't my doing. The seamstress thought it would be fun for our costumes to smell like the sweets we were going to portray."

"Oh." I stood there, awkwardly rubbing the back of my head.

At that moment, the Spanish dance ended with a final little flourish. "Guess it's time!" Mina whispered, her eyes sparkling as the lights on stage began to dim.

I was prepared to blow everybody away with this performance, including myself. However, Mina and I had barely made it on stage when the comments began from Lindsey.

"Ms. Gaskell, is that really how they're supposed to come in?"

"That's not proper technique, is it, Ms. Zeigler?"

"Why is her belly showing? Isn't that inappropriate?"

Halfway through our routine, she had gotten on everybody's nerves so much that Ms. Gaskell banned her to the wings. I had hoped that this would allow Mina and I to finally focus on our performance, but I was wrong. Standing just off stage, Lindsey was whispering loudly to her friends.

"Did you see her pointe work? I can't believe they even gave her the Arabian. She'd be better as a gingerbread kid."

"I can't believe she has the nerve to try to be an upstart."

"She thinks she's such a prima donna!"

"Ignore them," Mina whispered as she performed a strenuous handstand on my outstretched arms.

I was about ready to whisper back that I wasn't sure how much more I would be able to listen to when Professor Zeigler had suddenly had quite enough. "OFF!" she barked loudly. "Von Ballen! Backstage now until your next dance routine. If you can't even show your fellow performers basic courtesy, you will not receive any in return."

Without the added distraction of Lindsey onstage, we were able to finish the rest of our routine with very little difficulty. With an affirming nod from Ms. Gaskell, we were both sent backstage to change, me back into the Nutcracker prince outfit and Mina into her Flower Corps costume.

"Hey," I said, gently grabbing her hand before she made her way back to the dressing rooms. "Look, um, I never got to answer your question properly earlier about how you looked and so, um, I just wanted to say that you look absolutely beautiful."

She froze, her cheeks turning very pink. She swallowed hard and let out a shy giggle. "Well, you don't look half-bad yourself, Sultan."

At that moment, I realized I was still holding her hand. Embarrassed, I quickly let go and excused myself to change. As I left, I looked back to see Mina staring after me, her cheeks almost the exact shade of red as her costume.

# 8. Drowning Sorrows

By the time we had gone through the performance a few times, perfecting the timing, lighting, and entrances of each dancer, it was nearly dark outside. Although most of the students headed home right after the end of the dress rehearsal, I asked permission from Ms. Gaskell to stay a little bit later to continue practicing. Since the doors from the auditorium leading out into the parking lot would open to the outside even when locked, she agreed to let me stay as long as I wished, under the condition that I didn't "destroy anything."

I had always felt that it was rather different dancing on a stage than in a studio. The sounds, the ambiance, just the whole atmosphere was so different. While a studio was calm and controlled, a stage felt raw and tense, filling me with a strange nervous energy. When I could, I loved being able to practice on the stage I would be performing on. The more familiar I got with the space, the more I would be able to use its atmosphere and energy to my advantage on the performance day.

After I had run through my routines for the third time, I suddenly heard loud, slow clapping. Jumping, I turned to see a figure slouched in the back row of the auditorium.

"Bravo," said a very familiar voice.

Squinting, I tried to see to the back of the auditorium. "Professor?" I asked slowly. Although I could have sworn it was her voice, her speech sounded different, more lethargic.

"Professor? Yeah, I'm a professor..."

Quickly making my way off the stage, I found her sprawled in the back of the auditorium, a large, suspicious flask clutched in her hand.

"Are—are you drunk?" I asked incredulously.

"Why?" she slurred with a hiccup. "Do I sound like I am?"

I sighed. "So much for keeping the auditorium clean..." I muttered to myself. Glancing at my phone, I realized that it was nearly eleven p.m. "How on earth did you even get in here?"

Rummaging through her purse, she giggled in a very undignified way. "Key," she proclaimed, pulling it out to show me.

I searched my brain for answers on how to handle this. Most college syllabi don't tell you what to do when your professor shows up drunk to your late-night practice session. "You're going to have a massive headache in the morning," I warned, taking a seat beside her.

"Headache," she repeated with a giggle. Suddenly, the smile faded, leaving a very broken expression on her face. "Headaches..."

"Professor?" I asked, confused.

"D-David had headaches," she murmured, a far-off look in her eyes. "He used to ignore them."

"David?"

"You—you remind me of him," she hiccuped, taking another swig from her flask. "He didn't like my drinking either. Funny, isn't it?" She took a long look at my costume. "You look nice."

I wasn't quite sure how to respond to that. "Um... thanks?"

"You dancing in something?" she asked, motioning to my Nutcracker costume that I had forgotten to take off.

"Yes, professor. *The Nutcracker*? The one you're directing and choreographing?"

"*The Nutcracker...*" she said faintly, her eyes wandering across the darkened stage. "I dance in *The Nutcracker.*"

I froze. "What?"

"Every year."

"Professor," I said slowly, "I don't mean this to be disrespectful, but you're really drunk."

"I danced it every year with David."

"Who is David?" I repeated, frustration beginning to creep into my voice.

"You remind me of him, you know?"

"Yes, Professor, you mentioned that."

"He was my Cavalier."

"What?" My ears perked up. "Was David a dancer?"

She let out a loud hiccup. "He was the best dancer." A fond smile flitted across her face. "He was my Cavalier and I was his Sugar Plum Fairy."

"When was this, Professor?" I asked quietly.

"Years ago..." she murmured. "We'd always dance together."

"Was David your..." I searched for the right word, "... partner?"

"My partner and husband. Until..." Her voice faded away and she looked very young and lost.

I racked my brain. I couldn't remember reading about a David. Heck, I hadn't even known that she was married! Suddenly, the memory of an old news story came floating back to my mind. "Professor," I said slowly, "is David the reason you stopped dancing? Is he the reason you only direct and choreograph now?"

"David..." she mused. "David had headaches."

I was about ready to inform her that she had already told me this piece of information when she continued.

"He always ignored them... until one day—" she let out a strange laugh, "—he couldn't ignore them anymore."

"What happened?" I prodded gently, my heart racing.

Her face fell and a vacant expression spread across her face. For a few moments, we sat on the stage in absolute silence, Professor Zeigler staring blankly out at the empty auditorium. When she finally spoke, her voice sounded small and scared like a young child. "He was having dizzy spells. He was worried about the lifts—he didn't want to drop me. I wanted him to go to the doctor, but he thought I was being silly..." She was silent for a moment before pressing on. "He passed out one night at a dress rehearsal in October. I assumed he just hadn't been eating enough or something. Just pushing himself too hard, you know?" She took another swig of whatever alcoholic beverage her flask contained. "I couldn't believe it when the docs told us. I thought it was somebody's idea of a joke..."

"What was?"

A strange expression spread across her face as she let out a whisper: "Cancer."

My blood ran cold.

"At first, they told us it was nothing to worry about; they just had to run some tests." She let out a laugh that turned into a sob. "When the doctor came back and asked us to sit down, I knew—" she gulped. "It was inoperable, incurable, untreatable." She shook her head and buried her face in her lap. "Why even tell us if the truth was that bad?" she said, her voice muffled.

I didn't know what to say. I didn't know what to do.

"He was thirty-one," she whispered.

"How—how long—" I tried to ask, but the words just didn't want to come out.

"December 2, 2002."

Suddenly, everything clicked. "It's the anniversary of his death," I breathed. "No wonder you're drunk..." Something else jumped to mind. "Professor," I said slowly, "someone once told me that you never watch performances of *The Nutcracker* anymore, you just choreograph them. Is that true? Is that why you weren't at my last performance?"

"No more dancing," Professor Zeigler muttered, more to herself I suspected than to me. "No more dancing..." She reached to take another swig from her flask but I smoothly snatched it away.

"I think you've had enough," I said firmly, although I could feel my palms sweating. "Let's get you home." Then, I realized that I had no idea how to get her home... or if it was wise for her to be home alone in this state. "Professor," I began slowly, "do you have a cell phone?"

"Sure do," she exclaimed with an oddly happy smile. Reaching into her purse, she fished it out and handed it to me. Luckily for me, she didn't have a password lock on her phone... and she had her sister on speed dial.

Roughly ten minutes later, I was carefully helping a very drunk Professor Zeigler out to where her sister's car stood waiting. "I can't thank you enough for calling me," Ms. Gaskell said gratefully.

"It's nothing," I replied, glancing at my professor who was now almost passed out in the back seat of Ms. Gaskell's small car. "I just hope she'll be OK."

Ms. Gaskell let out a sigh and her shoulders slumped. "She—she will be. She does this every year. It's how she copes, I think." With a last warm pat on the shoulder, Ms. Gaskell hurried to her car.

As I watched them drive off, I couldn't help but wonder what it must have been like to not only lose your long-term dance partner but also the love of your life. Shuddering, I realized I didn't want to know.

# 9. The Show Must Go On

I didn't see Professor Zeigler again until the morning of the performance. Like any other major production, we all had to arrive at the auditorium by nine, even though the performance didn't start until seven that evening. The morning was spent in a flurry of activity as we went over (yet again) important safety announcements such as "Don't stand too close to the edge of the stage" and "Don't touch the mechanisms surrounding the Christmas tree prop." The younger dancers needed to be reminded once more where exactly they needed to enter the stage and their positions for scenes such as the entrance of Clara's godfather, Drosselmeyer.

The younger students were sent home during the lunch break while the more advanced dancers stayed to run through all of their parts once more. I saw Professor Zeigler throughout the afternoon as she triple-checked everyone's performance to make sure it was perfect for that evening. I wondered if she even remembered our conversation two nights before, but if she did, she gave no sign of it.

In fact, she almost completely ignored me. Usually, I would have been thrilled to be able to practice without my instructors nitpicking my every move, but today it just felt... wrong. I wondered if she was thinking about dancing or remembering David. Or maybe she was just thinking about how she wouldn't "be able to make it to the performance tonight."

Ms. Gaskell, on the other hand, appeared to have decided to adopt me. From cheering me on during my solos to pointing out how much my jumps had improved, it seemed I could do no wrong. Not that I was complaining. After countless hours and weeks of practice, I was relieved and encouraged to know that all of my work had finally paid off.

Perhaps, this performance I would actually dance in a manner truly worthy of Tchaikovsky's great piece...

Around four o'clock, we were all dismissed to go eat dinner with a strict warning to be back at the auditorium by 6:00 to start warming up and getting ready. As I grabbed my bags to head out, I felt someone staring at me. Looking up, I noticed Professor Zeigler watching me intently, a strange look in her eyes. With a little smile, I gave her a wave. As she gave me a sad smile in return, I realized with a heavy heart that the next time I saw her, *The Nutcracker* season for me would be over. She would never see the product of everything that I had worked so hard for at her urging. I wondered, if she saw me tonight, whether she would regret picking a lanky university sophomore to dance as her Nutcracker.

With a pang, I realized I would never know.

The next few hours seemed to drag by. It reminded me of being a kid on Christmas Eve. Like everybody else, I knew the whole story that "Santa won't come unless you're sleeping." And, probably like almost every other kid, sleep was always an elusive fantasy that seemed to stretch that night to an eternity. As I watched the time creep by before the performance, I realized that, a decade later, I was really no different than that kid waiting for Santa to come.

For the last few months, I had immersed myself in the world of *The Nutcracker.* Now that the night was here, the anticipation and nerves threatened to overpower me. Finally, at about 5:30, I couldn't take it anymore. Heading back out into the cold December weather, I returned to the auditorium to start practicing. As soon as I laid my hands on the barre, a sense of relief rushed through me. I knew this—this was familiar, comforting. As I moved through my warm-up routines, confidence slowly began to fill me.

I knew this. I could do this.

"Hello?"

Turning around suddenly, I saw a young man probably a year or so younger than me with meticulously combed black hair and thick dark-rimmed glasses. He was standing at the door of the room we had transformed into a private practice room, tightly clutching a small wrapped Christmas gift.

"I'm sorry to bother you, but I believe I am lost," the young man said with a very distinct New England accent. "I'm here to watch my girlfriend dance in *The Nutcracker,* and I thought I was in the right spot but now, I'm not so sure."

He looked nervous, standing there fiddling with the carefully wrapped gift in his hands. With a twinge, I was reminded of how I felt interacting with Mina. I glanced down at my watch; I had been so engrossed in my practice that I didn't even realize it was already 6:20. I hesitated. I still had about ten to fifteen minutes before I needed to be in costume...

"No worries!" I smiled. "You're in the right building, just on the wrong side of the stage." I chuckled as a confused expression spread across the young man's face.

"You're backstage where all of us performers warm up and change costumes and stuff," I explained. "Come on—I'll show you where you need to be."

"That would be incredible," he admitted with a sigh of relief as we set off down a corridor. "I just flew in from Boston, and I was really worried I was going to be late. I told her that I wouldn't miss this performance, and I was so worried that I had really botched this up again..."

"Hey, man, it's OK!" I said encouragingly. "Look, I bet any girl would be thrilled if their boyfriend flew in to see their performance. And I'm sure she'll be really touched by your gift."

Turning another corner, I saw the entrance to the auditorium. "Here you go—the seating area is right through there. If I were you, I'd try to sit about halfway up in the auditorium, maybe just a little closer to the stage. It should give you the best view."

He gave me a grateful smile and held out his hand. "Thanks, you don't know how much I appreciate this."

"No big deal!" I replied, shaking his hand.

He turned to head through the door but paused. "Good luck out there!" he added with a wave goodbye.

"Thanks!" I replied, returning the wave before heading back towards the dressing area. I glanced at my watch: 6:40. I cursed myself under my breath; I really should have been in costume almost ten minutes ago...

For once, I was grateful that Professor Zeigler wasn't here.

# 10. The Land of Fake Snow

I hate snow.

Before you go and get mad and start singing "White Christmas" and all that stuff, let me clarify: I love real snow.

I hate fake snow.

Specifically the fake snow used in the Land of Snow scene.

In the story of *The Nutcracker*, the innocent heroine, Clara, receives a gift of a Nutcracker from her godfather Drosselmeyer (don't ask me why—I'm not the one who thought a nutcracker would be a good idea for a kid!). Her little brother doesn't like the Nutcracker and ends up breaking its arm; since there are parents and other adults around, Clara decides not to break her brother's face in return and settles for just being tragically heartbroken.

Anyways, Clara stays up too late and falls asleep under the Christmas tree... at which point, the story starts to become a little weirder. Clara's toy nutcracker miraculously comes to life and starts battling an army of mice. Yes. You did read that correctly: mice. They are led by the Nutcracker's nemesis—the illustrious Mouse King (very original name). The Nutcracker and the Mouse King start fighting and Clara, in a panic, throws her little slipper at the Mouse King.

Apparently, slippers need to come with warning labels, because this one ended up killing the evil Mouse King. The mice eventually scurry away, bemoaning the demise of their fierce leader, leaving Clara with a wounded Nutcracker. Somehow, Drosselmeyer (who apparently has trained as a Fairy Godmother or something) helps Clara to break a curse on the Nutcracker and he transforms into—you guessed it—a prince. The prince is so grateful to Clara for "saving" him that he decides to take her to his kingdom. Along the way, they decide to pause their journey in the Land of Snow... And then they decide to dance a romantic Grand Pas de Deux with snow falling around them.

Usually, this is a breathtakingly gorgeous scene that helps to wrap up the first act of the ballet while setting the stage for Act 2 and the budding romance of Clara and her Nutcracker. On the other hand, usually the Snow Pas de Deux isn't danced by an awkward college student and a very whiny Coppelia[2].

"Careful!" Lindsey hissed under her breath to me as I lifted her up smoothly into a twist, a beautifully fake smile plastered across her face.

The performance had gone decently well up to this point. The young dancers had all (mostly) remembered their cues and had performed well for their ages. I was actually able to dance half-tolerably in the giant Nutcracker head. Lindsey appeared to be charming the audiences, and so far each routine had been met with a considerable amount of applause. Ms. Gaskell, at any rate, seemed pleased as she silently cheered for each dancer from the stage wings.

Truthfully, the Snow Grand Pas de Deux was the routine I had been dreading the most. Technically, it was a bit flashy and showy of a performance, but it wasn't the level of difficulty I was despising.

It was having to make the audience believe that I cared at all about Lindsey Von Barbie.

"Smile more!" Lindsey whispered, squeezing my hand more tightly than necessary as she danced "lovingly"

---

2 This is a reference to the titular character of the ballet *Coppelia,* which chronicles the story of a realistic, life-size doll.

around her Nutcracker.

Dancing is really another form of acting. Like a stage performer, you put on a mask, a facade. You become another person entirely for the purpose of telling a story to the world. Usually, I relish the freedom this brings. Dance allows me to express myself at a deeper level by transporting me to another world.

However, as I danced, my eyes trained carefully on Lindsey, I didn't feel like I was connecting with anybody at a deeper level. Despite all of my practice and work, I still felt mechanical as I spun her around. I tried to picture her as Clara, reminding myself that my Nutcracker was fond of her. But no matter how much I tried, I couldn't seem to muster the emotions. As we moved from pirouettes to leaps to even more pirouettes, I just felt...

Empty.

As I attempted my best to showcase Lindsey's talent as Clara, I realized that I was very different from the Nutcracker. The Nutcracker Prince was posh and suave and honorable and well-liked. Me? Well, I was about to blow my shot at having an absolutely stellar performance because I couldn't act like I loved the tolerably pretty teenager in front of me. I was awkward and clumsy and too blunt sometimes for my own good.

I was no prince.

The routine seemed to drag on forever, time frozen beneath the harsh cold lights and the gently falling pieces of white foam...

Have I already mentioned that I despise fake snow?

Sure, it's pretty when you're sitting in the audience, but when you're up on stage, it just gets everywhere. It gets in your hair, your costume, your face. It gets all over the stage and can make it slippery if you're not careful. But I think what I hate most about fake snow is its artificiality.

I love snow. I really do. I love having snowball fights and making snowmen. I love getting that amazing text or email saying that school has been canceled. I love running through it and the beautiful, strange, silent stillness that always seems to accompany a heavy snow. But most of all? I just like to watch it gently falling, gradually covering my familiar world in a white blanket.

The snow we use for our performances lacks that. It doesn't convey the beauty and serenity that real snow brings. To me, the fake snow, although a necessity, highlights that what we do up on stage is not truly real. It is merely a facade—a role to amuse others with.

As the music gracefully faded away, I smoothly lifted Lindsey up until she was perched on my shoulder. To those in the audience, we were a pair madly in love. The kind prince was gently lifting up the innocent Clara so she could better see the snowflakes.

As I danced, a fake smile plastered across my face, I realized that I was no better than the annoying white fluff falling around me. Lindsey's fingers entwined around mine as I mechanically lifted her down, reminding me once more of the artificiality of our predicament.

We truly were in the Land of Fake Snow.

# 11. Dancing With Fire

Have you ever watched fire? Flames have such bright, passionate beauty. They flicker and glow, dancing in the heat they create. They lap up everything they touch, consuming everything in their fierce desire. Their beauty is electric, intoxicating, and ensnaring...

Honestly, fire was probably one of the farthest things from my mind as I ducked off the stage during the entrance of the Spanish dancers—unless I was contemplating burning Lindsey with it. By the time I was finally allowed to escape from her greedy clutches, I was seething. No longer did I care about impressing any talent scouts or adding to my pathetic resume. All I wanted this Christmas was to never have to see Lindsey Von Barbie ever again.

She reminded me of one of those creatures who could sense fear... except with me, I think all she sensed was intense apathy and dislike. I had hoped that after the conclusion of the Snow Grand Pas de Deux, we would be able to mostly ignore each other and work our way through the rest of the performance. Boy was I wrong. It was as if my lack of passion during our climactic sequence had rekindled her determination that we should be passionately in love on stage and off.

As soon as the Spanish dancers made their entrance, I bolted. I could feel Lindsey's cold glare on the back of my head as I ducked backstage, but frankly, I didn't care.

According to Ms. Gaskell and Professor Zeigler's estimations, I only had about three minutes to change and be ready to perform. Hastily, I tore off the prince's stifling outfit and scurried to change into the Arabian Sultan's simple costume. As I quickly pulled on my pants, I recognized a strange, familiar smell. Looking around, I suddenly realized that the costume-maker must have made my outfit smell like coffee as well to match Mina's...

If I had more time, I probably would have been slightly upset that my manly outfit had been perfumed, but I was definitely running late. Throwing on the golden arm bands, I raced back to the stage where Mina was already dressed and waiting.

"Am I late?" I whispered, attempting in vain to catch my breath.

"No," she muttered back, fidgeting with her bangled bracelets. "They're just about at the halfway mark."

I let out a low sigh of relief. "You OK?" I asked suddenly, taking in her strangely pale face and her nervous pacing.

She jumped a little. "What? Me? No—I mean, I'm fine," she stammered with a strained smile.

"Really? You could've fooled me," I said sarcastically, shaking out my legs as I waited for our cue.

"I guess... I'm just nervous," she admitted, tucking a stray piece of hair back behind her ear.

I froze. "You? Nervous?"

She let out a little chuckle. "Silly, right?" She sighed. "It-It's just that there's a talent scout out in the audience and I really need this and—" She hesitated.

"Hey," I said softly, awkwardly placing my hand on her shoulder. "It's going to be OK. Seriously." I chuckled, mostly to myself. "Look, I know this may sound kind of corny, but you're the best dancer here. You can totally outdance everyone out there, and the talent scouts will see that."

"Well, I don't know about the *best* dancer," she murmured quietly, her hazel eyes meeting mine as a small smile danced across her lips. Suddenly, the room felt very hot and still. I became acutely aware of a strange buzzing in my ears and of my hand still resting on her bare shoulder...

"Uh-I-uh..." I stammered, moving my hand from her shoulder to rub the back of my neck. "I'm not *that* good, I mean—"

"Riolo, Durand!" Ms. Gaskell suddenly hissed, motioning us over. "You've got one minute. Into position!"

I looked back at Mina, who looked even more pale. "You ready?" I asked gently, reaching my hand out to her.

She looked back at me, a faint blush spreading across her face. "Ready," she replied determinedly as she took my hand.

We hurried over to the edge of the stage. Peering out from behind the curtain, I watched as the Spanish dancers twirled in time to the music. Lindsey was out there too, sitting smugly on the gold-painted prop throne as she watched the "sweets" perform for her. Quickly kneeling down, I helped Mina get into her first position. Professor Zeigler always liked dramatic entrances and the Arabian Pas de Deux was no exception. Don't ask me why, but Professor Zeigler had decided that the best way to introduce the Arabian coffee was to have the female lead perched on the shoulders of the male lead. Apparently, it was eye-catching... or something like that.

Nimbly, Mina hopped up onto my shoulders. Carefully, I stood up, making sure not to sway Mina too much. I could feel her tense up, and I chuckled. "Don't worry. I'm not going to let you fall."

She laughed quietly. "You'd better not!" Adjusting her position, she bent down until she was level with my ear. "Oh and Ben? That costume looks really good on you."

I could feel my face turn red as she giggled. The sound of applause brought me crashing back to reality as the Spanish dancers ran nimbly off the stage. As the audience died down, I watched as the lights changed from the bright, organized chaos of the Spanish variation to the dim, blue lights that signaled our entrance. "Hey," I whispered up to Mina, not daring to attempt to look up at her. "Forget about the scout. Just pretend you're only practicing with me."

At that moment, the sound of stringed instruments put an end to our conversation. Taking a deep breath, I smoothly moved onto the stage, carefully balancing Mina on my shoulders. Once I was standing before Clara's throne, I gently helped Mina climb down from atop my shoulders. Simultaneously, we bowed low before the throne, showing our respect to the Sugar Plum fairy and to our "savior."

I kept my head bowed resolutely, not meeting Lindsey's cold glare. I knew she was still miffed that I was dancing with someone other than her, but I didn't care. For once, I commanded the stage with someone other than her. This moment belonged to Mina and me.

And I wasn't going to let her spoil that.

Taking Mina's hand, I moved with her into the first position... and then I don't exactly know what happened.

Suddenly, the stage darkened and I could only see Mina. It was as if the audience and the other dancers in the production had just vanished. The music continued though, sweet and sad and seductive. The tune of the violins rang clear and mysterious across the empty stage, as if telling the world a story. For a moment, I wondered whose story the melody was whispering, but instantly, Mina seemed to appear in front of me.

Swiftly, I moved into our next position as we simultaneously pirouetted away from each other. Moving silently, we came close again, as though teasing each other. As Mina drew near once more, I suddenly felt as if the world was moving in slow motion. It reminded me of when I had first practiced with her but somehow... different.

She was stunning, I realized yet again as I watched her quickly move into a very difficult pointe position. Her red, sequinned outfit sparkled in the cool lights; every feature of her seemed perfectly chiseled, captured for eternity under the enchantment of the stage. She must have felt my stare because her beautiful eyes met mine, a small, teasing smile spreading across her lips. In an instant, she was in my arms as I smoothly picked her up for a lift.

For an instant, our faces were merely inches apart. Before I could do anything, she was gone again, moving into a pirouette. Following along with the music, I gently wrapped my hands around her waist as she began to flip her body smoothly over mine until she was behind me. I could feel her breath on the back of my neck, and I wondered if she could feel the heat that was now threatening to consume me. Gracefully, she slid her body between my legs, eventually coming to a standing position in front of me. I gently lifted her up by the waist until her arms were wrapped tightly around my shoulders. Panting, she leaned her body back until her feet and head were almost touching.

The music seemed to swell, drawing us into its exotic passion. Her face was hardly a breath away from mine and her cheeks were flushed, although if from exertion or from something else, I did not know. Her skin was hot and smooth against mine, the entrancing smell of coffee filling my brain. Her lips parted and her eyes began to close as I felt our bodies move closer...

At that moment, thunderous applause shattered my illusion. Blinking in confusion, I noticed that I was still on the stage. Mina quickly grabbed my hand and we bowed before hastily making our exit.

"Well done!" squealed Ms. Gaskell to us. As Mina replied back to the compliment, I leaned over with my hands on my knees. My head was still spinning, my breath ripping through my chest like daggers. I could feel the sweat dripping off of me, and I saw someone as if through a fog hand me a water bottle. After a couple quick gulps from the water bottle, I began to be able to see again, although my vision still had an odd, yet not unwelcome, red hue.

"Go on!" Ms. Gaskell hissed at me as Mina grabbed my hand. "Get back out there!" At that moment, I realized that there was a sound in the background I didn't recognize. Through my daze, I thought it sounded like rushing water. Quickly, I followed Mina back onto the stage, more than happy to be holding her hand. As I entered into the spotlight and glanced back out into the audience, I realized what the strange sound was.

Every person in the audience appeared to be standing, cheering.

For us.

# 12. In Her Eyes

The rest of the performance flew by in a blur.

I honestly don't remember much of the performance after the Arabian Pas de Deux. Hazily, I can remember dancing with Lindsey again, although I'm pretty sure she just glared at me the entire time. I can also vaguely recall the finale in all its regality and splendor. It really wasn't until I ran out onto the stage at the end of the performance during the curtain call that the moment really hit me.

As the curtain drew to its final close, I let out a long sigh of relief—*The Nutcracker* was over.

"Well done."

A familiar voice caused me to spin around so quickly I nearly whacked one of the younger dancers off her feet.

"Professor Zeigler?!" I asked incredulously as the dark-haired ballerina made her way through the crowded backstage.

"What? I can't congratulate the star of the show?!" she snapped, brusquely marching over to me.

"But... you—" I stuttered, not sure how to articulate everything I was feeling in that moment.

"Good work, Riolo," she grunted approvingly, her eyes blinking back what I could have sworn were tears.

"You came," I finally managed to get out, a gigantic grin spreading across my face.

Professor Zeigler rolled her eyes. "Well, obviously. I did choreograph it after all!"

I had no words. All I could do was just reach out and pull her into a tight hug. She just stood there frozen for a good minute or two before finally hugging me back. Pulling away, she hastily cleared her throat. "Careful, Riolo. You're ruining my image."

At that moment, I caught a glimpse of auburn out of the corner of my eye. Instinctively, I turned, craning to see where the star of the show had vanished to.

"Go on."

I glanced back at Professor Zeigler, who was now standing with her hands perched on her hips, a mischievous smirk flitting across her face. "You heard me," she continued, using her best "teacher voice." I felt

84

my cheeks get hot. "HA! You're blushing, Riolo!" she teased. Grabbing my arm, she leaned down to whisper in my ear. "You know? You two reminded me of how—how David and I used to dance."

I froze, my heart racing.

"It was magical." She gave me a genuine smile and a gentle push towards where Mina had vanished. "Go get her, Riolo. You two are perfect together. You're meant to dance together."

Swallowing hard, I gave her a quick nod, not completely trusting my voice at that moment. After another moment of hesitation, I turned quickly and made my way through the crowd of giggling students and their proud families.

Pushing my way past a group of middle schoolers, I headed further backstage in the direction I last saw Mina heading. Quickly, I searched through the eager faces of the performers, looking for the girl who had changed my life. As I searched, I began to panic as I tried to decide what I would say to her when I finally found her. I mean, what *can* you say after that kind of performance? It was, as Professor Zeigler stated, truly "magical."

As I made my way through the hallways and corridors, I began to see fewer and fewer performers. I had just been ready to head back towards the auditorium, thinking that I must have missed her in the sea of people, when I heard her dainty giggle.

Rounding another corner, I finally saw her in the empty practice room I had warmed up in before the show. She was still dressed in her Arabian costume but was now holding a large bouquet of crimson roses that seemed to perfectly accentuate the colors in her outfit. I felt a blush rise to my cheeks as I was once more taken aback by how stunning she truly was. I wondered if I was ever going to get used to that...

Somehow, I doubted I would.

Standing beside her was an older couple that I assumed had to have been her parents and a short young man with dark glasses who looked oddly familiar...

"Mina!"

She turned, a faint blush creeping across her face as she waved to me.

"I—I just wanted to say, um, that you did a good job out there," I stammered, my ears turning red as I felt the eyes of her entourage fixed on me.

"Thanks," she said softly. "You too."

The older man standing next to Mina cleared his throat. "Mina, aren't you going to introduce us?"

Her cheeks reddened. "Sorry, this is Ben Riolo. He starred as the Nutcracker and was my partner for the Arabian Pas de Deux."

I reached out politely to shake the gentleman's hand.

"Ben, these are my parents," she continued, motioning with a small smile to the older couple next to her. "And this—" she hesitated for barely a moment before smoothly continuing, "—this is my boyfriend, Chris."

I was sure I must have misheard her.

"We've met!" Chris exclaimed, extending his hand to shake mine. "This is the guy who helped me when I was running late and showed me where to sit."

I smiled mechanically, my mind racing.

"Good job out there!" the smiling young man congratulated me as he casually slid an arm around Mina's waist. "You've really got talent!"

"Thanks," I said, a strange tightness building in my chest.

"Mina," her mom tapped her on the shoulder, "we really need to head out if we want to make that dinner reservation."

Throughout this conversation, the girl of my dreams had resolutely been looking anywhere but at me. With that polite little smile I had come to know so well, Mina nodded to her parents. After a moment's hesitation, she turned back to me, still not meeting my gaze. "Well, Ben, thank you. It-well-it—" she stuttered, her cheeks turning red. "It was great. Best of luck with your career and thanks for helping me and everything."

I felt frozen. This must be a nightmare.

She turned to leave, her boyfriend and parents already a few steps ahead of her.

"Mina, wait!" The cry burst from my lips unbidden.

She looked back at me, her beautiful coffee-colored eyes meeting mine. In that moment, I saw into her soul. Where I found confusion in my mind, I saw a heartbreaking clarity in hers. Yet, the pain and agony I felt so acutely I saw reflected in her eyes, a testament to what we shared... and what she was throwing away.

I wanted to speak, to tell her everything I was feeling. I wanted to beg her, to plead with her. I saw a question in her eyes, and her lips parted as if to say something.

"Come on, Mina!"

The moment was gone.

She bowed her head as I began to realize she must have known this moment would come all along. She lifted her head once more, her auburn hair slipping from its bun and falling in loose ringlets around her beautifully sculpted face.

"Goodbye," she whispered, tears shimmering in her beautiful eyes.

"Mina—"

Turning, she ran to catch up with her family, leaving me alone in the empty practice room.

Leaving me as alone as I had been when I first met her.


Why am I writing this?

Why do I voluntarily dredge up such memories?

As far as why I am writing this... I am writing to remember. Someday, when my limbs can no longer carry me through the movements and rhythms of dance, I want to remember the emptiness of that room, the sounds of the families leaving, the emotions. I want to remember the feelings of sorrow, of passion, of pain.

I want to remember her.


What do you think of when you think of Christmas?

I think of the smell of coffee.

# Author's Note

*The Smell of Coffee* is actually inspired by real events. Many years ago, I attended a performance of *The Nutcracker* with my dear friend Lydia. We were a pair of broke college students and nabbed the tickets from a shady website for a bargain. We congratulated ourselves, assuming we had scored a deal on the local professional ballet troupe's performance.

On the day of the show, we realized we only had an address for the performance without any information on parking. When we arrived at the venue, there were no signs to point us in the right direction, and we ended up getting hopelessly lost. Somehow (to this day, I don't even know how!), we ended up backstage near the practice rooms. As we fumbled our way through the nondescript corridors, we bumped into a young man holding a Christmas present who became the inspiration for Chris. Thankfully, we did eventually find our way to the auditorium and to our seats mere minutes before the show was about to start.

To our surprise, the performance was not the professional ballet troupe we thought it was, but, rather, was a collection of performers of all ages. The performance was charming, whimsical, delightful... and hysterical. We had no idea why, but the teenager playing Clara sulked the entire performance. She had absolutely no chemistry with the Nutcracker, and had us giggling the entire time.

And then it happened: The Arabian Pas de Deux. The same young man who performed as the Nutcracker had quickly changed outfits and was dressed as the Arabian sultan, but his performance now was a far cry from the painfully awkward dances with Clara. He and his partner stole the show with their sensual performance, by far outdancing every other performer in technique, style, and passion. When the music drew to a close, the audience was still for a moment before we all jumped to our feet, giving the pair the only standing ovation for the night (with the exception of the final curtain call).

After the performance, my friend and I discussed the differences between the passionate Arabian Pas de Deux and the stilted Snow Grand Pas de Deus. We were both intrigued by the variety of the characters on the stage and wondered at their stories. At the end of the night, we challenged each other to write our own version of what led to that performance that night.

I hope you enjoyed my take and don't hate me too much for the ending. Thank you for reading.

# Acknowledgements

You know, after daydreaming for years about getting to write one of these, it's kind of tricky to know where to begin. There have been so many people who have helped make this moment a reality.

First of all, I want to thank *you*—the person reading this. Thank you for reading my work and for helping me to be able to pursue this passion of mine. It means more to me than you will ever know.

The biggest of thanks goes to my husband and best friend, Jonathan. He has been my biggest supporter, my rubber duck, my encouragement, and my protector. Without him, I honestly never would have gotten this out for all of you to read. I don't have words to tell y'all all the cups of tea he made, all the questions he figured out answers for, all the candles he's lit, all the breakdowns he circumvented, and all the love he shows me on a daily basis. Thank you for everything, you goober. You're the love of my life, and I'm so thankful to get to go on this crazy journey with you.

Next, I need to thank my other three big inspirations. Sophia, James, and Ruth—you three are too young to read this yet, but I want you to know that I love you all so much. Thank you for taking naps so I could work on this, and for being so patient when I steal your dad for long logistics and creative babbles, especially when y'all just want to go play with him. Thank you for being such awesome kiddos. Never give up on your dreams.

A special thanks to my parents for encouraging me to read and write tales from a young age. Thank you for giving me access to countless books and for teaching me to love stories. I love you both.

Thank you as well to the best in-laws a girl could have —Paul and Diane, y'all have been such an encouragement to me throughout this whole process. Thank you for all the prayers, feedback, and love you've shown me. I love y'all!

I must also give a special shout-out to my three beta readers: Lydia, Brenna, and Carys. Y'all are true MVPs. Thank you for reading this in early stages, final drafts, and everything in between. Thank you for your encouragement, threats, and love. Lydia, thank you for supporting this idea from the beginning and for attending that wacky performance with me a decade ago (wow, I feel old now!). Brenna, thank you for your ~~threats~~ encouragement, and for your complete belief that the world would love this story as much as you do. Carys, thank you for all your ballet know-how, your kindness, the indie bookshop runs, and your contagious excitement when I told you that I was going to publish this as a paperback.

A special thanks as well to Tim McKay for his amazing edits and encouragement! I appreciate your work and your excitement for the future of this story. If any of you reading this are authors/writers and need a good editor, Tim's fantastic. This book is so much the better for all his hard work.

Thanks as well to Piarul Islam Pias and his design team for the amazing cover! Piarul and his team were incredible to work with, and I highly recommend them in the future. They can be found on Fiverr under the name @anjoleena_26.

A well-deserved shout-out to my ARC readers—y'all are amazing, and I can't thank you enough for reading this early. You're the best!

I also must thank Bergmann School of Dance for allowing me to observe the intricacies of running a local dance school on a weekly basis. If any of you readers are in or around Weatherford, TX and are looking for a wonderful dance school, please look no further. I can not say enough good things about Angie and the lovely school she runs.

Thank you as well to Pattea Lou's Tea Room. Your amazing Butterbeer tea has helped me throughout the layout design process of this book and is probably the reason I still have hair. Y'all are amazing!

Finally, I also want to thank my grandparents and grandparents-in-law for their encouragement and love throughout this whole project. Grammie and Poppop—Thank you for encouraging me throughout it all, for keeping your eyes out for artists, for telling your friends and library about my work, and for refusing ARCs so you can buy it yourselves. I miss you and love you both so much. Grandpa and GrandBetty—thank you for reading my projects, for getting excited with me over new releases, and for all the wonderful lunches at Buttermilk Cafe. I love you both.

None of this however would happen if it weren't for the Creator of the universe. I am so humbled and awed to get to tell the stories He places in my heart. *Soli deo gloria!*

Until next time, dear reader. May your hearts be full, your lives joyful, your teacups steaming, and your bookshelves full. Thank you for reading.

# ABOUT THE AUTHOR

A. M. Burk was born in Pennsylvania, raised in upstate New York, and now calls Texas her home, where she lives with her husband and three children. A lifelong storyteller, Abigail has had short stories featured in local anthologies and served as a narrative lead for a video game company before stepping away to focus on her family and her own writing career. Her kids constantly inspire her and love to tell her exactly which of her stories she is writing next. She is the author of the picture book *Princess Marie and the Pesky Piper* (co-authored by her then-three-year-old) and the romance novella *The Smell of Coffee*. In addition, she's working on her debut novel and a plethora of upcoming children's picture books. When she's not writing, you can find her playing with her kiddos, taking care of her zoo of animals, bookbinding, playing video games, jamming out to musicals, playing piano, knitting (yes, like what your granny used to do!), and hanging out at local independent bookstores. Connect with her at her website (www.amburk.com) or follow her on social media (@authoramburk) for updates!

# Coming Soon: *The Stolen Veil*

An old German folk legend tells of a fairy maiden who had the ability to transform into a beautiful swan only if she was wearing her magical veil. Eventually, a man discovers her secret and steals her garment, exposing her true self for all to see. Although Arianne Gaskell would be the first to brusquely tell you that she was no fairy, the young prima donna ballerina eventually grows to realize how similar she is to the woman in the tale when she agrees to star in an upcoming production of *Swan Lake*. As she attempts to navigate potential rivalries within the troupe, a life-changing opportunity, and a handsome guest artist, Arianne grows to wonder who she really is beneath

the veil: the innocent, sorrowful Odette or the passionate,
dark Odile...

# Coming Soon: *Rosemary and Lilies*

Have you ever regretted a decision that has grown to haunt you? Have you ever found yourself wishing for another shot at changing your past? Eight years after the events of *The Smell of Coffee*, Mina Durand may just get her chance. When a beloved mentor convinces her old flame Ben Riolo to dance in an upcoming rendition of the ballet *Giselle*, Mina is left to wonder if the now prestigious choreographer will remember her, let alone forgive her for walking away from him so many years before. In a story of regret, heartbreak, loyalty, and second chances, follow Mina and Ben as they reconnect for a retelling of *Giselle* that no one will soon forget.